# *Lendercide*

a murder mystery

Allen Madding

Charm House Publishing

Saint Petersburg, FL

**T. Allen Madding/Charm House Publishing**
**Saint Petersburg, FL**
**www.charmhouse.pub**
**www.AllenMadding.com**

Publisher's Note: This is a work of fiction. Names, characters, places, and incidents are a product of the author's imagination. Locales and public names are sometimes used for atmospheric purposes. Any resemblance to actual people, living or dead is completely coincidental.

Editor: Priska Jordan
Book Layout ©2021 BookDesignTemplates.com
Cover Design ©2021 BookCoverDesign.Store

Ordering Information:
This book is distributed by Ingram, One Ingram Blvd., La Vergne, TN 37086. www.ingramcontent.com

**Lendercide/ Allen Madding**. -- 1st ed.
ISBN 978-0-578-86037-4
Library of Congress Control Number: 2021903106

# Acknowledgments

Special thanks to my wife Allison for coining the phrase "lendercide" which gave me the idea for this story.

Many thanks to my editor Priska Jordan for your outstanding work and continued support.

Continued thanks to my friends and family that regularly encourage me to keep writing

*An angry woman is vindictive beyond measure, and hesitates at nothing in her bitterness.*

–JEAN ANTOINE PETIT-SENN

"J ackass!" Colleen Smithwick screamed to no one in particular. She ran her fingers through her salt and pepper streaked brown hair and squinted her green eyes as she listened to the tersely worded voicemail on her desk phone. Colleen has been working overtime and skipping lunches to try to keep up with the avalanche of loans she was trying to process. Ever since she had come to work at Sunshine City Bank, it had been a never ending grind. And this was the last straw with this pushy and arrogant loan officer. She was trudging through five loans that were closing this week, and she wasn't about to take crap off of Richard Shiver. Hell might not know the fury of a woman scorned, but Richard was about to find out who he crossed this time. Today wasn't the day.

"Maybe if you provided all the information I needed, I could complete your damned package. I swear on all that is holy that man is going to make me commit lendercide. I have had more than enough of that pushy butt wipe."

Still fuming, she pounded the numbers for Richard's extension.

"What's the status of my loan package?" he quipped when he picked up her call. "I need docs so I can close tomorrow morning."

"Well, Dick," she started purposely substituting the common short name for Richard which relayed her thoughts on his personality. "I am

still waiting on the proof of insurance and disbursement information that I requested two days ago. Have you sent me those items?"

Colleen thought she heard crickets.

"Dick, are you there? Hello? Have we got a bad connection?"

She tapped the phone receiver on the side of her desk three times.

"Hello?"

Richard began to stutter.

"I...uh...I guess I forgot about that."

"Oh, I see. I am working on 20 other loan packages while I am waiting on you to provide me with what I need to complete your docs and send them to review, but you'll leave me another one of your nasty voicemails wanting to know when the hell I am going to get you your docs, huh? Well, you're lucky you're not in the office, because I would walk down to your office and hit you in the head with one of my shoes, you jackass! You get me the outstanding items, and we will discuss when you can schedule closing. But you can bet your ass it ain't gonna be tomorrow. Got it?"

Richard continued stuttering. "Um...yeah. OK. Let me call the client and see if I can get that together."

"That sounds like a great plan, sunshine," she said before slamming down the phone.

"Prick!" she shouted to no one in particular.

She resumed working and tried to calm herself down. While she worked, she began to imagine creative ways that Richard might meet his demise. She could run him over with her car. No! She loved her Maserati, didn't want blood on the body work, and there would be way too many witnesses. She imagined putting a bullet right between his eyes. Nah, bullets were too expensive to waste on someone like him, and ballistics were too easy to trace. She thought about a scene she'd seen in a movie long ago where a killer had snuck in behind the victim and strangled him with a piano wire. Her husband played guitar, so she had easy access to guitar strings. She wondered how much strength it would take to pull that off.

When she looked at the clock on the phone, it was 5:15 already. She hadn't noticed anyone leaving yet, but she realized that it was definitely quieter than usual. Time to leave before someone stopped her. Colleen clocked out, stood up, and grabbed her purse and the unopened Coke sitting on her desk. The phone started ringing again, but Colleen ignored it and walked out. "They can leave a message and wait 'til morning," she said out loud to herself.

When Colleen stepped out of the house to start her short commute to the bank the next morning, it was pouring rain.

"Typical Florida day," she thought. "It will rain for 30 minutes then stop, and the sun will come out and the humidity will be off the hook."

The rain set an ominous tone to the start of the day. She carefully maneuvered the flooding streets until finally reaching the bank parking lot. When she pulled in, she noticed what looked like remnants of barricade tape on the trees on both sides of the driveway and a couple of unfamiliar cars. Upon further inspection, she saw they all had city government license plates and black steel wheels with small, chrome-center hub caps.

"Undercover police cars," she noted as she crossed the parking lot. "I wonder if we had a break in last night."

As she walked into her office, she could hear muffled voices down the hall in the boardroom. She dropped her purse in the bottom drawer of her desk, logged into her computer, and hastily scanned the 70+ emails in her inbox before grabbing her coffee cup and heading to the break room. She poured herself a cup of coffee and dumped six creamers and two tablespoons of sugar into the mug, giving it a quick stir before heading back to her office. Halfway down the hallway, her

manager, Elena Vasquez, called her name from the boardroom doorway.

"Funny," she thought, "she's never here this early."

Colleen walked to the boardroom.

"Yes?" she answered.

"Colleen, the city police homicide detectives are here investigating a murder that took place in our parking lot last night. They are wanting to interview all the staff," her manager explained.

"Murder?? What the hell?" she replied.

"Mrs. Smithwick?" a blonde, blue-eyed, and well-tanned man she estimated to be in his early thirties dressed in a suit with a pink flamingo tie called to her.

"Yes?" she replied slowly.

"Mrs. Smithwick, I'm Detective Gary Black with the Saint Petersburg Police Department. We would like to ask you a few questions. Please come in and have a seat."

Colleen sat down across the table from the detective making firm eye contact.

"How can I help you?"

"Are you familiar with an employee by the name of Richard Shiver?" he asked.

"Yes, of course," she answered quickly. "White male, 40-something, condescending, rude, disrespectful, but moderately successful. I know him."

Stunned at the response, the detective scribbled on his notepad.

"We discovered Mr. Shiver's body in his car here in the bank parking lot last night. The medical examiner estimates that he was killed around 6 PM. What time did you leave work, and where were you afterwards?"

"Let's see," she said, recalling the events of the close of day. "I believe I left around 5:15. I drove over to KFC, picked up some dinner, and then drove home."

"Alright," he responded as he wrote. "How would you classify your relationship with him?"

"In a word," she answered, "arduous."

The detective furrowed his brow.

"I'm sorry. Come again?"

Colleen smirked at his lack of vocabulary.

"Arduous," she repeated. "Involving or requiring strenuous effort; difficult and tiring. You know, taxing, difficult, exhausting, fatiguing, bordering on intolerable."

The detective continued to scribble on his notebook.

"Do you know of anyone that would have a reason to want to see him dead?", he asked without looking up.

"Hmm," she replied, "that would be a long list. Like anyone that ever had to deal with him. So, the entire loan processing staff, the tellers, the people that service his Mercedes, the people that pick up his dry cleaning, the staff at Starbucks, his ex-wife. Yeah, pretty much anyone unlucky enough to cross his miserable self-absorbed path."

The detective slowly raised his head, "You included, I take it?"

"Yes," she dragged out the word. "Yes, I am one of the poor souls that had to endure his narcissistic existence, so that makes me one of your suspects along with about 100 other people in Saint Pete that were unfortunate enough to have to endure his charming personality. They don't let us carry here, so my 9mm Sig Sauer is locked in my car if you would like to run ballistics on it. It hasn't been fired since last weekend, but you are welcome to test it."

"That won't be necessary," the detective replied to her offer. "He wasn't shot."

Colleen tilted her head to one side. "Oh?"

"Yes, ma'am.," he continued. "Oddly, he was stabbed to death."

"Well, there's a small pocket knife in my purse if you would like to test it."

"That won't be necessary either," he dryly replied.

Colleen seemed confused by his response.

"Ma'am, frankly, he was stabbed in the neck with a metal letter opener. Quite accurately, he was stabbed in the jugular vein. Just one stab wound to a very vital area. Do you have a letter opener?" he asked.

"No," Colleen answered. "I don't process any mail. That all happens down on the first floor by branch staff. I don't think I have even seen a metal letter opener in 15 or 20 years."

The detective laid his pen down on his notebook.

"OK, ma'am. We're checking the camera system and computer system to verify when everyone left and if his car was in view of the parking lot camera. We'll verify the information you've provided. If we have any further questions, we will be in touch."

He pulled a business card from his jacket and handed it to her.

"Here's my card. It has my cell number on it if you think of anything that might be helpful."

Colleen took his card and glanced at it. She smiled.

"I was going to ask you for your number, but I didn't think it would be professional," she said with a wink.

The detective smiled and then casually noted the diamond on her left hand as she turned and walked out of the boardroom doors.

Colleen returned to her office and turned her attention to the pipeline of loans. Of course, the voicemail light on her desk phone was illuminated, Microsoft Teams was showing 14 missed messages, and her Outlook inbox showed 86 unread messages.

"Could I be left alone long enough to prepare one of these loan packages?" she thought to herself.

She clicked the icon for the Loan Processing software, and an error message popped up on the screen.

"I really don't have time for this nonsense right now," she said out loud.

She promptly dialed the bank's IT help desk. When one of the help desk guys answered the phone, she immediately recognized his voice.

"Daryl, I'm getting an error trying to open the Loan Processor. I have 30 loans to work and loan officers raising hell they can't close them all tomorrow."

"Good morning, Colleen," Daryl replied calmly. "What's the error message?"

She read him the message and a long code that looked like a hexadecimal number.

"I hope that means something to you."

He chuckled. "Sounds like it can't communicate with the server. Give me a minute."

Colleen heard the bank's hold music start. She started reading and deleting emails. She swapped screens and replied to several Teams messages and then back to email again. After a few minutes, Daryl came back on the phone.

"I rebooted the server. Let's see if that got it for you."

She clicked the icon, and the Loan Processor program opened.

"Yup. Once again you have saved the day. Thank you."

"You're welcome," Daryl replied. "If those loan officers get out of line, give me names, and I'll adjust their attitudes. I'm tired of hearing them abusing you."

"Thanks, Daryl," she said, hanging up the phone.

## 3

E lena was reviewing loans when Brad Stuckey stepped into her doorway while lightly tapping his knuckle on the door.

"Elena," he began, "Hammerstein is a friend of the bank. The loan we're processing needs to close tomorrow."

Elena glanced up from her computer screen to meet his stare as he took a long sip from a bottle of Mountain Dew.

"Well, Colleen has six closings she is working on. I am almost certain that Hammerstein is number five, and there are three loans scheduled to close tomorrow," she responded.

Brad shook his head. "No matter. Hammerstein closes tomorrow. Also, it looks like we're behind on ticklers and getting out Adverse Action notices. Make sure those get caught up immediately."

Elena took her glasses off, set them on the desk, and looked him in the eyes.

"Well, Brad, it seems you have competing priorities. You want us to rush a large loan while trying to complete the ones we are already working on, and you'd like us to stop working on loans and address ticklers and adverse action letters. Which is the most important?" she asked.

Brad's ears turned crimson red.

"I want all of it done as soon as possible. All of it is important. I don't care if you and Colleen have to work 24 hours a day, seven days a week. Get it done. Are we clear?" he vented.

"Crystal," Elena snorted in response.

Brad sharply turned on his heels and disappeared down the hall.

"Good riddance," she thought to herself.

She picked up the phone and buzzed Colleen's extension.

"Colleen," she said, "Brad wants Hammerstein to close tomorrow, and he is harping about ticklers and adverse action letters."

She drew a breath and waited for the response. She thought that she heard choked back tears.

"Um. Well, how am I supposed to do that? It's 2 PM, and I am already going to be working late trying to finish the three that close tomorrow. I'm just one person. I haven't even had a lunch break in two months. I can hardly even run down the hall to pee," Colleen responded despondently.

"Just focus on getting Hammerstein ready. Don't worry with the ticklers and adverse action letters. Let me see what I can do about those," Elena suggested.

"I'll do my best, but at some point I am going to need a break. I can't keep on like this!" she said as she began sobbing uncontrollably before hanging up the phone.

Elena looked back up at her computer screen and noticed an instant message from one of the loan processors. She clicked the message and hastily scanned it.

"For the love of God, now what?" she said out loud to herself.

She quickly typed a response. Within seconds, a woman with salt and pepper hair and steel gray eyes appeared in her doorway.

"How can I help you, Margaret?"

"I wanna take off next week. I've worked overtime every night for a month and each of those Saturdays. I think I should get some comp time for it," Margaret demanded.

"Margaret," Elena began as she ran her fingers through her dark hair. "First, I can't give comp time in a separate week from the time worked. Secondly, we have got so much going on, we really can't afford for anyone to be out."

Margaret stiffened her jaw. "Well, if you can't see me having a week off, I can always just quit."

Elena sighed. "How about you take PTO Friday and Monday?"

Margaret snorted. "That's the best you can do?"

"I can give you Friday as comp time and you take PTO on Monday. Brad was just in here ripping and roaring that he wants ticklers and adverse action letters done, so that's about as good as I can do right now," Elena bargained. "I need you to start working on the adverse action letters between the loans you are processing in the meantime."

"Fine," Margaret replied emphatically. She turned and stomped back down the hallway.

Elena picked up her phone and buzzed Lori's extension.

"Hey, Elena," Lori answered.

"Lori. What's your pipeline looking like right now?" Elena inquired.

"I have two closing on Friday and another I just received. What's up?"

"I'm going to need you to help Margaret."

"Help her to AA?" Lori responded with a smirk.

"Not funny," Elena quipped. "She is going to be out Friday and Monday, so check with her if she has anything closing or pending. I need both  of you working on adverse action letters. We're behind, and Brad's on the warpath."

"Great," Lori replied. "I love working with the old battle axe."

Elena hung up the phone and then buzzed Neil's extension.

"Hope you're having a marvelous day, this is Neil. How can I make your day more fabulous?" he answered.

Elena rolled her eyes.

"Neil, I need you to start working on ticklers. We need to make sure we don't get caught with expired documents if auditors pay us a visit. Brad says we're seriously behind on addressing them. So, between working on the loan packages for your lenders, I need you to go through all the current files and ensure ticklers are set."

"Alright," Neil answered, "I'll try to make some time tomorrow to begin looking at that."

4.

Around 5 PM, Colleen heard a light knock on her door and glanced up from her work to see Brad standing in her doorway.

"Hey, Colleen. I'm running low on Mountain Dew again. Could you pick some up for me tonight?"

Colleen could feel bile in the back of her throat as she answered him, "Sure."

"What was he going to want next?" she thought. "Pick up his dry cleaning? Shop for his wife's birthday? Do I look like his personal assistant? Jackass!"

It was 7 PM when Colleen pulled into the carport of the modest 1940's bungalow she shared with her husband of 15 years. She walked in and headed straight to the master bedroom. She kicked off her black stiletto heels with the red soles and tossed them in the bottom of the closet. She unbuttoned her blouse, slid it off her shoulders and tossed it in the hamper. She unsnapped the strap in the center of her bra and unholstered her Sig Sauer P365 9mm pistol and placed it on the bedside table before removing her bra, slacks, and thong and tossing them in the hamper. All the banks in her career had forbidden

employees from carrying weapons, but after a robbery at one of her former banks, she wasn't taking any more chances.

She stopped in front of the dresser mirror and gazed at her reflection. The years had been gracious to her. No sagging breasts and just a little more than a flat tummy. She turned around and glanced at her butt over her shoulder. She hated the small wrinkles of stubborn cellulite on her upper thighs that she struggled to work off. Her husband always complimented her on her legs and encouraged her to wear skirts and bikinis, but she always shied away desiring to hide her thighs. She grabbed a pair of yoga pants and a t-shirt and slid them on before walking to the front of the house to the living room.

As she walked into the living room, her husband, Alex, set down his tablet and stood up from his recliner to greet her.

"Welcome home, dear," Alex said. He wrapped his arms around her and held her tightly and gave her a kiss. She halfheartedly kissed him and sighed. A graying dachshund raised his head from the dog bed next to Alex's chair and shook his ears.

Colleen knelt to rub the old dog's head. "Hey buddy. Have you been good today?"

Alex chuckled. "Oh yeah. Except for the two times he snuck out of my office and peed on the dining room floor while I was on conference calls."

Colleen shook her head.

"How was your day?" he asked.

"Long, obviously," Colleen started. "On top of the giant stack of loans they're rushing to close, when I got to the bank this morning, the parking lot was filled with cop cars. They found Richard dead in his car in the parking lot with a letter opener impaled in his neck."

Alex's eyes were the size of saucers. "What in the holy hell happened?"

Colleen shrugged. "No idea, but it couldn't have happened to a nicer guy," she said with sarcasm dripping from her lips. "I never would wish ill on someone, but if I did, he would have been high on the list."

"Do the cops have any suspects?" Alex inquired.

"Oh, just the entire loan operations staff at this point. We all hated the pompous jackass," she answered.

"Wow. Glad I'm not a detective," Alex replied. "I took the liberty of ordering dinner from Outback. I knew you'd be exhausted. It should be here in the next 15 minutes or so."

"Thanks," she replied.

"How about a glass of wine or something?" he asked, stepping toward the liquor cabinet.

"Sure. Wine would be great," she answered.

Alex poured her a large glass of her favorite blush and handed it to her as she stretched out on the sofa to read.

olleen arrived at the bank the next morning, verified the all clear signal, and proceeded up the elevator. She stopped by the break room and slid two six-packs of Mountain Dew bottles into the refrigerator.

"Ungrateful little prima donna," She said to herself.

She walked into her office, turned on some classical music, and returned to preparing loans documents for closing. It was around 11 AM when the branch manager came running upstairs to Colleen's office doorway.

"Call 911!" he said breathlessly. "We've just been robbed!"

Colleen snatched up the receiver on her desk phone and quickly dialed 911. She began relaying details. After several minutes, she hung up the phone and dialed Alex on her cell phone.

"Hey dear," she greeted him. "We've just been robbed. I am OK. That's all I am allowed to say. I'll tell you more when they clear us to go home."

"I love you, babe," Alex said. "Stay safe."

Colleen hung up the phone and stepped into the hallway. She could hear commotion downstairs. Looking out the hallway window, she could see the bank was surrounded in crime scene tape and police cars.

Elena approached her where she was standing.

"The police and FBI agents are downstairs interviewing the branch staff and completing their investigation. One of the tellers was pistol whipped and is being transported to the hospital. Everyone is safe. The guy just walked in, walked up to the teller line, pulled a pistol, demanded money, and struck one of the tellers in the forehead with the pistol," Elena reported.

"Crap!" Colleen snapped. She could feel her pulse racing and began trying to control her anxiety.

"Once the FBI and police have completed their investigation and interviews, we'll be sending everyone home for the day," Elena concluded. She gave Colleen a hug and turned back to the hallway to brief the rest of the operations staff.

Colleen did her best to compose herself. She returned to her office and tried concentrating on her work to distract herself from the situation. Around 1 PM, she heard a light knock on the door and looked up to see Elena.

"Management has brought in lunch for everyone since we are still being held captive by the police. There's soup, salads, and sandwiches in the break room."

"Thanks," Colleen replied.

Finally, at 2:45 PM, an announcement came across email and the phone intercom system that the bank was closed for the remainder of the day and all staff was dismissed.

Colleen texted Alex: "We're dismissed. On my way home."

She hurriedly logged out of her computer, grabbed her belongings, and headed home.

When she walked in the door of their house, she noticed the lighting was dimmer than normal.

Alex met her in the bedroom. "I've ran you a bubble bath, lit some candles, and poured you a glass of wine. I'll be in my office working if you need me." He kissed her cheek and quietly headed back down the hallway.

Colleen undressed and walked into the bathroom. Classical music was playing and candles flickered a warm, relaxing glow. She slid into the tub, leaned back, and closed her eyes.

The water in the tub began to slowly cool when her cell phone vibrated. She reached to the side of the tub and picked it up to read the message.

"Hello, Mrs. Smithwick. This is Detective Black. I had a few additional questions in the murder investigation of Richard Shiver. Could we set a time to meet and discuss?"

Colleen grinned as she read the text and pictured the handsome detective in her mind. She raised her knee above the soap bubbles and took a selfie carefully positioning to prevent any bare skin other than her bent knee, arms, and face. She sent the picture in reply to the detective with a note. "I am currently indisposed, but maybe we could meet over drinks after work tomorrow." She smiled at her playful flirtatious move.

After a few moments, her phone vibrated again. "6 o'clock tomorrow evening at Bonefish Grill?"

She smiled again. "That's fine," she replied and then deleted the conversation to prevent her husband from finding it. She rose from the tub, dried off in an oversized towel, and donned her fluffy hotel robe.

## 6

The following morning Colleen stress level was off the chart as she rushed documents to four lenders for closing that had been rescheduled due to robbery and early branch closure. In the middle of the rush, the loan processing system went down.

"DAMMIT ALL!" she shouted.

She snatched up the phone and called Daryl from I.T.

"Daryl, Loan Processor is down, and I have the sharks circling here. I need some help and fast!" she blurted out.

"Take a deep breath," Daryl replied calmly. "I'll reboot the server. It will take a few minutes for it to come back up. While we are waiting, breathe. In through the nose, out through the mouth. Close your eyes. Relax."

Colleen rolled her eyes and took a deep breath.

"That's a start," he commented. "You're buddy ,Brad, decided to target me this week. I knew he was rough on the Loan Operations team, but I guess he wanted a pound of my flesh, too. He won't let us have the budget to upgrade our systems, but he's bent out of shape that they go down under high demand. Seems like he wants to have his cake and eat it, too."

Colleen nodded. "Sounds about right. He wants what he wants whether it's practical or possible."

"Yeah," Daryl said, "someone needs to readjust his attitude. OK, looks like the Loan Processor server is back up. See if you can access it."

Colleen clicked the icon and the program opened.

"Yup. Thanks."

"You're welcome," Daryl replied. "Hope you day improves."

"It won't," Colleen replied.

A little after 5 PM, Colleen looked up when she heard her name called and saw Lori standing at her door.
"I'm headed out. I think Elena is still here," she said.

"OK, thanks," Colleen replied. "I'm not going to dally much later. I have to be out of here by 5:30."

Lori smiled. "Hot date?"

Colleen laughed. "Something like that."

"Have a good night," Lori said.

"You, too," Colleen answered.

At 5:30 PM, Colleen promptly logged out of her computer and hurried to the ladies' bathroom. She used the toilet and then set up shop at the large vanity. She opened her purse and retrieved several items. She touched up her makeup, reapplied bright red lipstick, and spritzed on some perfume. She checked her hair and then unbuttoned the top three buttons on her blouse before heading out to meet Detective Black.

She carefully scanned the bar area when she stepped in the door of Bonefish Grill. She spotted the detective seated at a high-top table at one end of the room sipping a drink from a rock tumbler. Her eyes lit up and a smile beamed across her face. She felt herself blush slightly as she made her way to his table.

He glanced up as she approached.

"Good evening, Mrs. Smithwick," he greeted her.

"Colleen," she replied. "How are you, detective?"

He smiled and responded, "Gary. Can I get you a drink?"

"That's fine," she answered. "Crown and Coke."

He held up a finger while looking toward a server who rushed to the table.

"I'll have another," he requested, "and the lady will have the same."

The server nodded and turned to the bar.

Colleen raised an eyebrow. "Nice coincidence."

"Good taste," he replied. "And from the photo last night, nice legs."

She grinned. "Well, thank you."

He nodded and raised his glass in a salute before taking another long sip emptying the contents. "I wanted to ask you a few questions," he said, patting his lips with the side of his index finger.

"OK," she replied. "Shoot."

"Are you aware of Richard Shiver having any romantic involvement with anyone at the bank?" he started.

"Richard?" she laughed. "Who would touch that irritating, self-absorbed jackass?"

He chuckled. "Maybe someone trying to get a promotion?"

She shivered at the thought. "Eww."

The server brought their drinks, and Colleen hurriedly took a long drink from hers as if trying to wash away the picture in her mind that had been painted by the detective's question.

"If there was, the only one I think of would be Lori, but hell, she flirts with every man in that office. It would be pretty difficult to tell if she would actually follow through with any of them."

He retrieved his notebook, made a quick note, and nodded as she spoke.

"What was his relationship with Marie like?" he asked.

She thought for a second while taking another sip from her glass. "At times it almost seemed like they were competitors for some bonus or incentive. I wouldn't say there was any bad blood between them, but at times it seemed like there was a bit of competition between the two."

"Alright," he said again, scribbling in the notebook.

"Why don't you tell me about you?" Colleen said, gazing over her glass.

"Oh?" he responded, looking up from his notes. "Not much to tell. 32, divorced. I live out at the beach. I run to reduce my stress and like to fish out on the gulf as time allows."

"Very nice," Colleen commented.

"And you?" he asked in response.

Colleen slightly blushed. "You know the profile specifics. I like a good trashy novel, walks on the beach, and traveling."

"And how is marriage?" he inquired.

She snorted. "Oh, it's there. He's a very nice guy that dotes on me. But I dunno, I get bored with it all. Sometimes I wish I could just run away and start fresh. I just don't feel the flames of passion for him like I used to..."

He nodded while sipping his drink. "Understood."

"So, why hasn't some hot little thing snapped you up?" she asked bluntly.

He laughed. "Well, I stay pretty busy with this job and after the divorce, I really haven't let myself be available for any commitments."

"I see," she replied coyly, "just playing the field."

"Something like that," he answered.

"Y'all got any leads on the robbery?" she asked.

"Major Crimes along with the FBI agents are reviewing video from inside the bank and the parking lot. From what I have heard, y'alls cameras are from the stone age. It's pretty tough to make out any details," he responded. "You'd think a bank would invest in some good cameras."

Colleen chuckled. "Not this bank. We ignore updating technology and just bitch about how slow and unreliable all the systems are."

"Sounds about right," he commented as he held up a finger to the server. "Well, that's all the questions I have at the moment. I'm sure you need to be getting home."

Colleen sighed. "Yeah."

"Check please," he said the server as she approached.

"Well, if you need anything else, you have my number," Colleen said as she began to stand up from the table. "Related to the case or personal. I'm a good listener, and I enjoy a good conversation."

Gary smiled in return. "Thanks."

As she turned and walked for the door, she could almost feel his eyes following her across the room.

olleen had been buried in her work when she heard movement and looked up to see Lori standing outside her doorway.

"Happy Friday!" she chirped.

Colleen had always wondered how anyone could be so damn chipper early in the morning. Did they pop out of bed with sunshine streaming out their ears?

"Happy Friday, Lori. How are you?"

"I'm fantastic!" she beamed.

"Of course she is," Colleen thought.

"So, how was your date last night?" Lori inquired.

"Oh that. That wasn't really a date. That detective wanted to ask me more questions," Colleen explained.

"You mean that tanned, sharply dressed, blonde detective?" Lori asked.

"Yeah. That one," Colleen answered.

"He's a hot one. Shame you aren't single. I noticed he kinda followed you with his eyes while he was in the bank," Lori noted.

"Pfft!" Colleen replied. "That's his job. I'm sure I'm not on his personal wanted list."

"Ya never know!" Lori said with a giggle. "Anyhow, have a good day."

"Yeah, you too," Colleen said, turning back to her work.

Colleen started to instant message Brad to discuss one of his loan packages she was finishing when she noticed he was offline. She flipped over to his calendar in Outlook and noticed he wasn't scheduled to be out of the office. She messaged Elena to ask if she knew where he was. Instantly her desk phone rang. She answered the call and heard Elena's voice.

"You are not going to believe this, but we just had a call a few minutes ago. Brad was found dead at his condo. The police and coroner are trying to determine the cause of death."

Colleen shook her head. "Whoa! Fly that by me again."

"Yeah, it was a shock to all of the management team as well," Elena continued. "The police said nothing had been disturbed in his condo, and there were no wounds or marks on the body."

"In a week's time, we have two dead lenders and a bank robbery," Colleen noted. "Is this place haunted or something?"

"Good question," Elena replied. "HR was planning on sending a grief counseling team this week, but they were delayed due to the robbery. So then they were going to send victim-of-violence counselors today, and we have another death."

Within an hour, Colleen saw detectives walking from the elevator past her office heading toward the boardroom.

"Oh, for crying out loud," She thought to herself. "Here we go with this again. I'm never going to get any of these loans done with all these interviews."

Slowly but surely, she watched the first floor bank staff file by her office for their individual interviews with the detectives. Just before noon, Gary showed up at her door.

"Hi, Mrs. Smithwick. Can we have a moment to talk with you in the boardroom?" he asked.

"That's fine," she replied.

Colleen locked her computer and followed him to the boardroom. She glanced down at his butt as he walked ahead of her and smiled.

When she entered the boardroom, Gary sat down in one of the chairs next to an older gentleman also wearing a badge on his shirt pocket. The older man stood and introduced himself.

"Good morning, Mrs. Smithwick. I'm from the coroner's office. We had a few questions, if you don't mind."

"Certainly," she replied as she sat down across the table from the two men. "How can I help?"

"We were wondering if you knew of any medical issues the deceased might have had. Heart trouble, diabetes, migraines, strokes, seizures, or anything along those lines?"

"I have no idea on any of that," she dryly replied. "We weren't close. I have no real knowledge of any of his personal details. I imagine when you begin to perform your autopsy you will either find ice water in his veins or piss and vinegar instead of blood. Was the house really cold, because I know snakes are cold-blooded animals."

The older man raised his eyebrows and slowly looked up from his wire-bound notepad. "I take it you weren't a fan," he noted.

"Affirmative. I'm sure I'm not the first that has checked the 'not a fan' box," she pointed out.

"No," he quickly replied. "He didn't seem to have been a candidate for Mr. Congeniality at your bank."

"Do you know of anyone he had any problems with?" Gary asked.

Colleen chuckled. "I think there is a staff directory by that phone there," she said, pointing to a sheet of paper with employees' names and telephone extension numbers. "That would be everyone he had a problem with at this branch."

"Duly noted," Gary replied. "Where were you last night, Mrs. Smithwick?"

Colleen's mouth formed a slight grin as she cut her eyes toward him. "Well, I had drinks at Bonefish Grill after work and then went home around 8:30 or so."

"Alright," he said matter-of-factly. "I have no further questions. Do you?" he said looking at the older gentleman.

"No, I'm good," the older man said.

"OK. Well it was a pleasure guys, but loans are waiting."

She stood up, smoothed her skirt, and walked out of the boardroom, all the while feeling Gary's eyes slowly trailing down to her stiletto heels with the red soles.

"Christian Louboutin," he thought. "How the hell does a loan processor afford Christian Louboutin shoes? And it's a different pair every time I see her."

He made some additional notes in his notepad before moving on to the next interview.

Colleen resumed her loan work. She was determined to get caught up on the packages that were delayed by the events of the week, so she skipped lunch, opting for a pack of peanut butter crackers and a Coke from the break room. Around 5:30 PM, Elena popped her head in the door of Colleen's office.

"OK. Shut it down and get out of here. We've done all we can do for this week."

Colleen looked up and noticed the time.

"Yeah, sounds goods" she replied. She wrapped up what she was working on, cleared the top of her desk, and logged out of her computer.

"I'm still shocked about Brad," Elena commented. "He seemed like he was healthy as a horse, playing golf all the time and out on his sailboat."

Colleen shrugged. "As much Mountain Dew as he drank, I wouldn't be surprised if he had a coronary. He walked in the bank first thing in the morning with one already in his hand, and he had me keeping the break room stocked with them for him."

"I guess it's possible," Elena noted. "Well, have a good weekend. Stay safe!"

"You, too." Colleen replied before heading to the elevator.

As she rounded the corner, she saw Lori waiting for the elevator.

"Hey girl, headed home?" Lori asked.

"Yeah, I've had enough of this week," Colleen replied with a sigh.

"Would you care to grab a drink before you go to the house?" Lori offered.

"Yeah, that would be nice," Colleen answered with a smile.

"Cool! Let's meet up at Proof. Fridays is ladies' night," Lori suggested.

"That's fine," Colleen replied.

She dug her phone out of her purse and sent her husband a text: "Going out for a drink with the girls from work. I'll be home later. Don't wait for dinner. If you're hungry, go ahead and eat."

As she stepped into the elevator, her phone vibrated with a response: "OK. Have fun and stay safe. I love you."

She abruptly typed in a reply, "Love you, too. TTYL," and slid her phone back into her purse.

When Colleen entered the cocktail lounge, she spotted Lori sitting on one of the couches. Lori looked up and waved her over.

"Plop down over here and get comfortable," Lori greeted her. "I just love these leather sofas."

A server walked over and delivered two drinks.

"I took the liberty of ordering for us. I think you will like this one. This drink is called the Zue South. It's a bison grass vodka with thyme, lemon, and soda water. I love it."

"Thanks," Colleen said as they clinked their glasses together.

She took a sip and was pleasantly surprised. "Mmm. That really is good!" she noted with a grin.

Lori handed her a drink menu.

"All their drinks are handcrafted specialties. You get to pick the next round."

Colleen sipped her drink and slowly reviewed the menu.

"The Rosalyn's Collins sounds good. Vodka with rose petal syrup, lemon, rosemary, and soda water. Hmm," she said, pointing to the entry on the menu.

"Ooh, that does sound delicious," Lori responded. "So what do you make of all this craziness this week?"

Colleen took a long sip and then set the glass on the coffee table in front of them.

"It wouldn't surprise me if they both were murdered by a disgruntled coworker, an ex-girlfriend, ex-wife, ex-boyfriend, or ex-lover. I have a hard time swallowing that Brad died of natural causes. I kind of wonder if someone slipped a mickey in his drink after work or something. You know neither one of them had a big fan following."

She picked up her drink and took another long sip.

Lori nodded in agreement. "They were both tyrannical assholes as far as I am concerned. I try not to wish bad on anyone, but there have been several times over the last year that I wanted to kill both of them."

Colleen nodded as she finished her drink. "Don't tell that cute detective this, but I actually have thought of ways to kill off both of them. Some are more graphic than others. Richard was such a prick, I started calling him Dick to his face. The day before he was murdered, I had wanted to take one of my shoes and drive the heel right between his beady little eyes. And he was such a disgusting little flirt. I even considered going out with him, taking him to his house, tying him up and choking his ass to death with a belt."

Colleen noticed Lori's eyes were the size of saucers.

"Wow!" Lori exclaimed, "I knew you were a tiger, but that is pretty intense."

"Sorry," Colleen said shyly.

"Don't be," Lori replied. "It's kinda hot," she said with a giggle.

"Oh, ya think?" Colleen replied as a server brought the second round of drinks.

"Absolutely!" Lori said smiling. "Well, you are pretty damn hot in those skirts and stilettos. The aggressive side is a nice addition."

Colleen beamed. "Well, considering the source, I take that as a pretty high compliment. Rocking that cute little 20-something figure."

Lori smiled. "I could kiss you for that."

Colleen leaned closer to her. "What's stopping you?" she said with a devious grin.

Lori leaned in and kissed her softly on the lips and leaned back to look at her reaction. Colleen was looking into her eyes with a smile.

"Is that the best you got?" she asked playfully.

Lori leaned in and kissed her again, parting her lips, and delicately sliding her tongue into Colleen's mouth. Colleen lightly chewed Lori's tongue and quietly groaned. Lori slowly ended the kiss and looked up at Colleen.

"Girl, you really are a tiger aren't you?"

Colleen giggled. "People underestimate my mild manner."

"I guess so," Lori replied. "I am glad I got to see under the veil."

"Oh yeah?" Colleen inquired.

"Hell yeah!" Lori replied. "We should hang out more."

Colleen smiled. "That could probably be arranged."

"It wouldn't get you in trouble with Alex or that cute detective, would it?" Lori asked.

"Pffft!" Colleen answered. "There's nothing going on with that detective."

"Yet!" Lori interjected.

"OK," Colleen relented, "yet. And as far as Alex, I can keep a secret as good as the next."

"Nice," Lori said, "because I could use more of those kinds of kisses."

Colleen giggled. "Well, there's more where that came from if you are smart enough to keep your mouth shut at work."

Lori nodded while sipping her drink. "Mum's the word, girl!"

Lori leaned in for another long kiss and gently slid her hand on the inside of Colleen's thigh. Colleen leaned into the kiss and placed her hand on top of Lori's hand to prevent it from going further up her skirt. When their lips separated, Colleen looked at Lori.

"OK, girl, I think I've had enough to drink. I probably should head home for the evening."

"Alright," Lori said, sounding slightly rejected. "Give me your number?"

"Sure," Colleen replied and dictated her number as Lori punched it into the contacts on her phone.

"I'll text you, so you can save me in yours," Lori suggested.

"Cool," Colleen said retrieving her phone from her purse. It vibrated in her hand as she picked it up.

"Hey ya, hot stuff!" the text from Lori read.

Colleen giggled as she stored the number in her contacts and deleted the message to ensure Alex didn't accidentally find it. She then texted him: "Paying the tab and heading your way."

ary returned to his cube at the Saint Petersburg Police headquarters. He listened to several voicemails on his desk phone and read through the emails waiting on his computer. The crime lab hadn't found any fingerprints on Richard Shiver's car, and the letter opener didn't have enough surface to fingerprint. Was there some kind of connection between Richard Shiver's murder and the death of Brad Stuckey? Was there any connection between the two cases and the bank robbery? It seemed too much action in one week to write off as coincidence. But what other thread connected all the events other than the bank?

He picked up his desk phone and called the Major Crimes Division.

"Hey guys, have h'all got any leads on Wednesday's bank robbery?"

"White male. Early to late 30s, 5'9" to 6', approximately 190 pounds, right-hand dominant, grey Hoodie, blue jeans, white tennis shoes. He left on a bicycle with approximately $2,500," the voice on the phone replied.

"That's it?"

"'fraid so," the voice continued. "No prints. We believe he was wearing latex gloves. The teller he struck with the pistol said it was a short barreled, black revolver. Not really a lot to work with. We're

yielding to the FBI on this one. It's a bank, so it's their jurisdiction. I've seen better quality video shot on disposable cameras, and we have no witnesses outside the bank. If the Fed's come up with any leads, we will pursue them, but until then…"

"Gotcha. Thanks," Gary replied and hung up the phone. He brushed his fingers through his blonde hair and retraced the interview conversations in his head. The robbery might very well be unrelated, but he was convinced that the two deaths were related. He re-checked his email for the coroner's report, but it hadn't arrived. He stood and walked a couple cubes over to another detective who had processed Brad's condo.

"Hey, Joe. Run down the scene at the Stuckey condo."

Joe reared back in his desk chair. "Let's see. We were notified by his house cleaner. She showed up and was surprised his BMW was still sitting in the driveway, and then she found the body. No forcible entry found. No wounds or any type of injuries on the body. No needle marks. No drug paraphernalia found. Honestly, it looked like the dude just died in his sleep. He was in bed in a pair of silk pajama shorts."

"So, nothing disturbed, nothing out of the ordinary?" Gary inquired.

"Nope," Joe answered. "We found his wallet with all his credit cards in it and $850 in cash. The key fob for his car was next to it. Condo was neat, tidy, and in order. We went through the car and didn't find anything of significance. Interviewed a couple of neighbors and his ex-wife. Nothing seemed to stand out. It's almost like he laid down and died in his sleep."

Gary nodded. "Any other time, I probably wouldn't think twice about it, but with the murder of another lender at the same bank and same branch during the same week…"

Joe nodded in agreement. "I hear ya. It certainly seems suspicious."

"Alright," Gary said. "I guess we have to wait for the coroner's report. Thanks, Joe."

"Yup," Joe replied, turning back to focus his attention on his computer screen.

Gary glanced at his smart watch and decided it was time to call it a day.

## 9

Colleen was feverishly working to ready two loan packages for closing when she heard a knock on her door. She looked up to see Gary standing in the doorway.

"Good morning, detective," she said with a flirtatious grin.

"Good morning, Mrs. Smithwick."

"I think we have been through this before. It's Colleen," she said somewhat dryly.

Gary closed the door behind himself and sat down in one of the guest chairs facing her desk.

"Colleen, I need to ask you a few more questions," he started. "Are you the person that was stocking the break room refrigerator with Mountain Dew for Brad Stuckey?"

Colleen wrinkled her brow.

"Yeah. He constantly was telling me to pick him up some more like I was his personal assistant or something. It was kind of degrading. I kept waiting for him to tell me to pick up his dry cleaning next. The smug little jackass."

Gary nodded.

"Once you bought the drinks, did they ever leave your possession before you placed them in the break room refrigerator?"

Colleen squinted her eyes trying to understand the questioning.

"No. I would pick them up at Publix on the way home from work, put them in the trunk of my car, and then carry them inside the next morning when I arrived for work. Is there something wrong with the drinks?"

Gary glanced down at the thick burgundy carpeted floor for a second, collecting his thoughts, and then looked back up at Colleen making direct eye contact.

"The coroner's original report didn't find anything out of the ordinary, but his family apparently has some heavy political influence with the mayor's office and demanded an in-depth toxicology report. Long story short, the coroner determined the cause of death to be ethylene glycol poisoning. So the crime lab tested all the contents of the refrigerator at his condo and came up with nothing. Over the weekend, they contacted your branch manager, and with his permission, tested everything in the break room refrigerator."

Colleen's eyes widened.

"And they found automotive antifreeze in the mountain dews in the break room refrigerator?"

Gary nodded.

"Precisely. At this point we are trying to determine how that came to be. We interviewed some of your co-workers earlier this morning. Margaret Prescott said she believed Brad was pinging you to buy them for him."

"Yeah," Colleen replied, "out of my own personal money, I might add. But I haven't tampered with any of them. I just bought them at the grocery store and tossed them in the fridge."

"Understood," Gary said, trying to calm her reaction. "We're just gathering facts and trying to assemble the pieces. From talking to her, it doesn't seem like there was any love lost between Margaret and Brad either."

Colleen smirked.

"There wasn't any love lost with him and any of the Loan Operations team. He was unpleasant to deal with on any transaction large or small," she noted.

"Any significant history between the two? Anything more than what the rest of y'all encountered from him?" he inquired.

"I recall several times she said that he called her an 'aggravating old bitch'. Needless to say, that didn't sit too well with her. I don't know if she ever took it to management or HR or whatever," she replied.

"Interesting," he noted. "OK. I won't tie up any longer. Thank you for your time."

Colleen smiled. "Who knows, detective? Maybe I might like to be tied up," she said with a wink.

Gary stood and let himself out of her office without a response.

He walked down the hall to Elena Vasquez's office and tapped his knuckles on the door frame.

Elena looked up from her computer.

"Good morning, detective," she greeted him. "How can I help you?"

"I wanted to ask you a couple questions related to the relationship between Mr. Stuckey and Mrs. Prescott."

Elena took her glasses off and laid them on the desktop next to her keyboard.

"Alright," she said.

"Did you ever hear Mr. Stuckey call Mrs. Prescott an 'aggravating old bitch'?"

Elena shook her head.

"He never said that in my presence."

Gary nodded.

"Did Mrs. Prescott ever come to you to report abusive language?"

Elena nodded.

"Several times. She reported him calling her that and several other derogatory remarks related to age and gender."

Gary scribbled notes on his spiral-bound notebook as she talked.

"Alright. Was any action taken related to her complaints?"

Elena's shoulders dropped as she sighed.

"I spoke to HR, but he was an Executive Vice President and a high producer for the bank. I don't know what they did with it, because personnel management is confidential. But, it seemed like he was the fair-haired child of senior management. Untouchable, if you will. As long as he was bringing in multi-million dollar loan packages, he seemed to do no wrong in their eyes."

Gary finished his notes and flipped his notebook closed.

"Alright. Thank you, Ms. Vasquez."

"You're welcome," Elena replied. "Pretty sure if you want any information from HR's side, you'll have to present them with a warrant."

"Yeah, so I figured," Gary commented. "Thanks again," he said before leaving her office.

Colleen walked into the break room around 2 PM to microwave some soup for lunch and saw Lori sitting at a table picking at a microwave meal.

"Just not feeling it?" she asked.

Lori chuckled. "Yeah, not so much."

Colleen sat down at the table across from Lori to eat her soup.

"So, they're saying Brad was poisoned with the Mountain Dews in the fridge here," Colleen said, tilting her head towards the break room refrigerator.

Lori nodded. "Yeah, so I heard. They aren't trying to pin that on you, are they?"

Colleen shrugged. "Well, I was the one that bought them and delivered them, so I guess I am prime suspect number one. You really have to wonder, though, how they got antifreeze in them when the bottles are sealed? Certainly Brad wouldn't have drank one with a broken seal."

Lori's eyebrows shifted. "Good point. I guess I won't be drinking any of the bank-provided bottled water from here on out."

"For real," Colleen replied. "Someone must have been pretty confident they would be able to get away with it."

Colleen began eating and scrolling through Facebook on her phone. When she finished scrolling through her notifications and the latest

posts, she decided for kicks and giggles to see if Gary had a Facebook profile. She quickly found it but other than his name and the current location of Saint Petersburg, Florida, everything else on his profile was set to private. She shrugged her shoulders and sent him a friend request. Within a matter of moments, she received a notification that she her friend request been accepted. She began slowly scrolling through his wall and his photos. She soon landed on some photos of him at the beach, shirtless in a pair of shorts. She squirmed a bit in her chair. She had a definite physical attraction to him that she could not deny.

Suddenly, her phone vibrated in her hand with a text notification. It was from Gary.

"What are you doing cruising Facebook? Aren't you supposed to be working?"

She grinned as she typed a response. "Late lunch break. I either read a book or scroll through Facebook during lunch."

"What kind of books do you like to read?" he responded.

"Well," she started. "I like graphic dominant/submissive novels."

"Oh really?" he replied. "A little fantasy for some role playing?"

She giggled.

"Well yeah," she typed. "I have fantasized about being a submissive. Some light bondage, spankings, etc."

"That's fascinating," he soon responded. "I would have never guessed."

She giggled again.

"You might be surprised what secrets hide below the exterior of your average working woman."

"Average?" he replied. "I wouldn't classify you as average."

She grinned a mischievous grin. She gathered her things and dropped them off at her desk before heading to the women's bathroom. She closed herself in one of the stalls, lifted her dress high enough to expose the dragon tattoo on her upper thigh and snapped a picture that just happened to include a bit of the black thong she was wearing, and sent the picture to him.

"NICE!" the response suddenly came back. "You're definitely not average."

Colleen giggled, dropping her dress, and exiting the stall. She checked her appearance in the bathroom mirror before heading back to her office.

"I hope that doesn't make it hard for you to concentrate on your work," she playfully replied.

"It will be hard," he replied, "but, I'll do my best."

Colleen returned to the loan packages requiring her attention. The share drive disappeared from her file explorer on her computer, as it seemed always occurred when she had a lot of work and was making good progress.

"For the love of all that is holy and good!" she shouted loudly enough for her co-workers to hear.

She snatched up the desk phone handset and dialed Daryl in I.T.

"Hey, Colleen!" he answered. "What's going on?"

"The share drive has disappeared again," she sighed, "right as I was trying to email a couple loan packages I had just completed."

"Alright," Daryl replied calmly. "Let me remote in, and I will remap them for you."

"Thanks, Daryl," she said graciously.

"No problem," he said. "Hey, I saw you out the other night but didn't want to interrupt."

"Really?" Colleen replied. "When was this? Where was I?"

"It was at Bonefish Grill. I was on my way out and saw you in the bar area. Looked like you were with that blonde detective that conducted all the interviews after the murder," he noted.

"Oh yeah." Colleen could feel her cheeks warm from blushing. "He wanted to ask me some more questions related to the investigation."

"Alright," Daryl said, "I got your drives re-mapped. See if you can access them from email now."

Colleen clicked her mouse a couple of times. "Yup, it's back. Once again you saved the day. Thank you."

"No problem," Daryl replied. "Always happy to help. Have a great afternoon."

Colleen hung up the phone and went back to work.

G ary strolled into the Saint Petersburg Crime lab and to the cubical of one of the technicians.

"Hi, Jan. What ya got for me?"

"Oh hey, Gary," replied a slender redhead wearing a lab coat. "The eight bottles y'all brought in from the bank's break room all still had the factory seal ring intact. So we put a couple under the microscope to see if we could find anything that would indicate how they were tainted. Upon examination, we found a very small puncture in the cap of every bottle you provided us, including the two we originally determined had high levels of ethylene glycol. After further examination, we arrived at the conclusion that the ethylene glycol was injected into the bottles using a hypodermic needle and syringe through the plastic screw-on cap. The needle was small enough that the casual, unsuspecting individual would not notice any tampering."

Gary took copious notes as she talked.

"So, an ordinary plastic syringe like someone would use for, say, insulin?" he asked.

"Not exactly," Jan replied. "Because the plastic bottle cap is more dense than human skin, an insulin syringe and needle would probably prove ineffective for this application. We'd be talking something like a syringe set for a cortisone. The suspect utilized a needle stiff enough not to break while penetrating the plastic cap but small enough not to leave an easily detectable disturbance to the cap. I'd have to speculate a fair amount of testing was completed to find the best choice. We're completing some further research to approximate the gauge of the needle, if that is helpful."

"Gotcha," Gary said as he finished his notes. "Would you estimate that it would require an above average grip strength to operate whichever syringe they used?"

"Nah," Jan answered. "If your grandmother could marinate a turkey, then she could have injected ethylene glycol into those drink bottles."

"Alright," Gary said. "Thanks. That's good information to work with."

He made some further notes in his spiral notebook before leaving the crime lab. As he walked, he opened his phone and pulled up the picture that Colleen had sent him. He smiled and shook his head.

"So freaking hot," he said to himself. "I'm going to have to interview her in depth, I believe."

He quickly typed a text to her: "Was wondering if you could meet me for dinner after work."

After a few minutes his phone vibrated, and he saw the response.

"I could probably make that happen. Say 6 PM? Where would you like to meet?"

He smiled and replied: "How's Carrabba's on 4th?"

She replied: "That's fine."

When 6 PM rolled around, Colleen walked in to Carrabba's to find Gary already occupying a booth in the bar section of the restaurant. She made her way to him.

"Hello, gorgeous," he said, looking up.

Colleen shook her head, dismissing the compliment. She slid in the booth across from him and folded her hands on top of the table. The server stopped by the table, and she ordered a peach sangria.

"What's on your mind, detective?" she inquired.

"Well, that tattoo for one," he replied playfully.

"Oh really?" she quipped. "So, you're thinking you need a closer inspection, huh?"

"Indeed," he replied, "I feel compelled to investigate every avenue."

She giggled. "I might be able to arrange that," she said, putting emphasis on the word "might".

The server returned with her wine, and Colleen took a long sip.

"How are your cases coming along?" she inquired.

Gary shook his head as he took a drink from his rocks glass. "Still chasing down leads and reviewing forensics. Kind of a wide field of suspects when you are as unpopular as those two."

Colleen nodded. "I could see that."

The server returned, and they ordered dinner.

"Does your husband know you are having dinner with me?" Gary asked, raising his eyebrows.

"Sort of," Colleen promptly answered. "I didn't say we were having dinner, just that you had contacted me and wanted to ask me some additional questions after work. I don't think he suspects you have any non-business intentions."

Gary smiled.

"I found your reading interests intriguing. Tell me what you like and fantasize about."

Colleen lightly blushed. "Well, I have a riding crop and like to be playfully spanked. I like light bondage, like being tied up with scarves or maybe even handcuffed. I like being blindfolded. Some of the things I have read lead me to think I'd like to experiment with dripping candle wax."

"Really?" he responded with intrigue.

She giggled again. "And you? What do you like? What are your fantasies?"

He took a long sip from his glass. "Well, I like spooning and sensual massage."

She smiled. "Very nice."

They finished dinner and Gary paid the check. "Would you care to come back to my condo for a night cap?"

Colleen grinned. "That's fine," she said as he held out his hand, helping her out of the booth.

They walked across the dark parking lot to his car. He opened the passenger door for her and she crawled into his car. He walked around the car to the driver's side when suddenly a figure darted out from the darkness and struck him in the back of the skull. His face hit the side of the car as he struggled to right himself. As he fumbled to find his footing, he felt cold metal pressed into his left ear and hot breath on the back of his neck.

"OK, pretty boy," the male voice said. "I know you think you're pretty slick swooping in on her and thinking you're gonna have your way with her, but that was your first mistake. And you're gonna pay with your life right here, right now."

Gary struggled to recognize the voice. He was sure he had heard it before. Before he could consider reaching his holster under his sports coat, he felt the man's hand pull his gun from his waistband. His mind was racing on what defensive maneuver he could attempt to break the man's hold now that he did not have a weapon.

Colleen popped out of the car and shouted, "Daryl!"

Gary suddenly recognized the name. Daryl! He was the computer guy from the bank. He was on Gary's suspect list, but he wasn't ranked very high. What the hell?

"Put the gun down, Daryl!" Colleen cried.

Daryl put one forearm around Gary's neck while still holding the pistol in his ear. "Don't try to defend this scum, Colleen. He's going to get what he deserves."

"Daryl, put the gun down, turn him loose, and let's talk."

Daryl shook his head from side to side. "Not happening, sweetie. Get back in the car so you don't see this."

With Daryl's attention focused on Colleen, Gary stomped the top of one of Daryl's feet and then kicked him in the knee cap. Pain shot through Daryl's leg, and he lost his grip on Gary's neck. Gary then gave him two quick jabs in the ribs with his elbow frantically trying to separate himself from Daryl and make some room between them and the side of the car. Daryl righted himself and took a quick aim at Gary's back.

A shot rang out quickly followed by a second shot. A woman getting out of a nearby car screamed.

Daryl felt a sharp pain in his chest. He grabbed his chest and recognized his shirt was warm and wet. His knees buckled, and he fell to the asphalt.

Sirens began to wail. Gary ran to Colleen who was still holding the Sig Sauer she had aimed at Daryl's body on the ground.

"Hand me your gun," Gary said reaching toward her.

Colleen removed her finger from the trigger, slid it alongside the side of the gun, and slowly handed Gary the pistol with the muzzle towards the ground. Gary ejected the magazine, cleared the barrel, and laid the weapon on the roof of his car. He then picked up his gun from where Daryl had dropped it and re-holstered it. He retrieved Daryl's gun from his loose grip, ejected the magazine, cleared the barrel, and laid it on the trunk of his car.

Within moments, the parking lot was full of police cars and an ambulance. EMTs loaded Daryl into an ambulance and whisked him away to the local hospital with red lights flashing and sirens wailing. Two officers handcuffed Colleen and placed her in the back of one of the police cruisers. Two detectives interviewed Gary while perplexed and curious restaurant patrons tried to figure out how to extricate their cars from the parking lot surrounded with police cars and crime scene tape.

After what seemed like an hour, Gary walked to the cruiser where Colleen sat silently replaying the events of the evening in her head. He leaned toward the partially cracked rear window.

"You alright?" he asked.

"Well," she started. "I've been mirandized, handcuffed, and tossed in the back of a police car like a wanted felon for saving your life. All things considered, I'd go with physically OK, emotionally pissed, and shaken up."

"I thought you liked cuffs," Gary playfully quipped.

Colleen cut her eyes at him and gave him a stare that instantly sent ice water running through his veins. The color drained from his face and his grin melted.

"I'll get them to uncuff you. But they're going to want to interview you downtown separate from me," he said.

"That's fine," she replied. "Can I at least call my husband and tell him I'll be late coming home. I think he at least deserves the courtesy."

Gary nodded. "How are you going to explain this?"

Colleen shrugged. "I haven't figured that one out yet. I think I have made a mess with him that's going to be hard to clean up."

Gary walked over to one of the officers that had handcuffed Colleen and had a brief discussion. The officer approached the cruiser and opened the back door.

"Mrs. Smithwick," he said. "I apologize for your being handcuffed. When we arrived, we were concerned with securing the scene and ensuring all the players were contained. I understand you saved a detective's life tonight. Our police force is indebted to you. If you will turn and face the opposite direction, I'll uncuff you."

Colleen scooted around in the cruiser seat exposing her cuffed hands to the officer who promptly removed them. She sat up in the seat and began rubbing her wrists.

"May I step out of the vehicle?"

The officer nodded. "Yes, ma'am, but the detectives would like to interview you, so please stick around."

"Understood," Colleen replied.

Stepping out of the cruiser, she glanced towards Gary's car. She noted all the handguns were gone.

"Probably bagged for evidence," she thought.

She walked to where Gary was standing.

"Can I get my purse out of your car?" she quietly asked.

"Sure," he answered as he walked her to the car and opened the passenger door. "Thanks for covering me there."

She grimaced as she retrieved her purse.

"You're welcome. It probably will cost me my marriage," she noted as she dug her phone out of her purse and stepped away from him to call Alex.

Alex sat in his recliner reading with a Chihuahua curled up asleep in a blanket in his lap. He sipped a Crown and Coke as he read, wondering when Colleen would come home. Since going to work for Sunshine City Bank, her hours had been long and grueling. He stood by helplessly watching the sparkle drain from her eyes and her glowing smile disappear from her mouth. The job was draining the life out of her and the joy from their marriage. He hated her job, and he resented the demanding, unappreciative, and self-centered lenders that she complained bitterly about every night. He wished he could somehow save her from the job and the emotional, physical, and mental damage it was having on her. He scheduled weekend getaways and vacations, but nothing seemed to improve her countenance.

"Bastards," he thought to himself.

Suddenly, his cell phone began vibrating on the table next to his recliner. He quickly picked it up and answered it.

"Hey, sweetie. You alright?"

He instantly recognized something wrong in her voice when she answered. "Alex, I am OK. There has been a shooting. I had to shoot a man who attacked the detective I was with."

"WHAT?" Alex shouted, awaking the dog in his lap.

"It's a long story which I will explain later. But Daryl, the I.T. guy from the bank, tried to kill the detective, and I had to shoot Daryl," she said.

"Holy mother of pearl!" Alex replied. "Is the detective OK? How is Daryl?"

She shook her head in disbelief as she related the situation to him over the phone.

"The detective is fine. I'm pretty sure Daryl is dead. I hit him twice center mass."

"Good girl" Alex commended her. "You're range time paid off. I am glad you and the detective are alright. Where are you?"

Colleen drew a deep breath knowing the answer would probably tip him off that something more had been afoot.

"I'm standing in the parking lot of Carrabba's surrounded by police cars and crime scene tape. The detectives want me to go down to the police station for a statement, so I'm guessing it will be late when I get home."

"Carrabba's with the detective?" Alex thought. "That's odd."

He dismissed the thought for a moment.

"Alright. Honey and I will be waiting for you when you get home. Be careful. I love you," he said.

"Alright," she replied and hung up.

"Not even an 'I love you'," Alex noted to himself, shaking his head in disbelief.

After two hours of answering questions and writing out her statement of the events of the night, Gary drove Colleen back to her car at the Carrabba's parking lot. When they arrived, she noticed the crime scene tape was gone, and the parking lot was virtually empty with the exception of a couple of employees' cars and her Maserati. Gary drove his Camaro close to where her car was parked.

"Here we go," he said.

Colleen looked over at him and squeezed his thigh. "Sorry things didn't work out tonight quite like we planned."

Gary snorted. "Yeah, not even close," he noted.

"Are they going to put you on administrative leave for being involved in a shooting?" she asked.

Gary shook his head. "Since I didn't fire my weapon, I won't be put on leave. I had to write a statement much like you did, and my supervisor wants me to submit to an examination by a psychiatrist for any mental or emotional trauma and an examination by my general physician for any injuries from the struggle. They took my sidearm and gave me a loaner to verify I did not discharge it. And, I'm

supposed to go from here to the hospital for a toxicology blood sample. Since I didn't fire my weapon, it's really a lot of formalities, comparing written statements - yours, mine, and witnesses, and comparing evidence gathered at the scene. Don't be surprised if one of the other detectives contacts you with follow-up questioning."

She nodded. "Understood. I better get home and prepare for another line of questioning."

She slid out of the passenger seat of his Camaro, stepped in to her Maserati, and headed for home.

Alex was dressed in his pajamas, sitting up in bed, when Colleen finally arrived home around 1 AM.

"Are you OK?" he softly asked.

"Yeah," she replied with a sigh, "I don't know what motivated it, but we were walking out of Carrabba's, and Daryl leaped out of the darkness behind Gary and put a gun in his ear."

"Maybe he had a secret crush on you and felt threatened by the detective?" Alex suggested.

She cut her eyes to him. "If he did, why on earth would he be jealous of Gary?" she replied.

Alex furrowed his brows. "Well, why were the two of you at Carrabba's?" he questioned.

"He just had some additional questions for his investigation and thought we'd handle them over dinner," she answered coyly.

"Colleen," he replied.

"What?" she asked innocently.

"Honestly," he continued, "why were the two of you at Carrabba's?"

"Seriously," she said, sticking to her story.

"Carrabba's has always been our place," he responded. "We know the proprietor, the kitchen manager, shift managers, and half of the servers. You don't think I got a couple texts from some of the staff asking why you were having drinks with a younger man and what was going on with us?"

The color drained from her face.

"There is nothing going on between us," she said defensively. "We're just friends."

He nodded. "OK, then can I see your phone?"

Colleen squinted her eyes trying to follow his request.

"My phone?" she asked.

"Yeah," Alex replied. "We have an honest and transparent relationship, right?"

"Right!" she said emphatically.

"OK. Then if there are no secrets, can I see your phone?" he requested again.

Her mind raced because she knew she had not deleted her latest conversation with Gary including the selfie she had taken in the bathroom stall that morning.

"Colleen?" he asked, noting her hesitation. "If you have nothing to hide, what's with the hesitation to let me see your phone? You know the unlock code on my phone. You know where it sits on the charger every night."

Her mind continued to race as she tried to find a way out of the corner she felt she was in. Her vision began to narrow, and she felt herself collapsing.

Alex grabbed her before she hit the floor as she passed out. He gently carried her to their bed and laid her down. He unstrapped the stiletto heels from her feet and set them at the foot of the bed. He dampened a wash cloth and laid it across her forehead. He had seen her once before pass out from anxiety and recognized the onset this time. While she fluttered her eyes lying on the bed, Alex reached into her purse and retrieved her phone. He punched in her lock code and drew a deep breath before opening her text messages. He clicked on Gary's name and scrolled up through the conversation landing on the selfie and accompanying messages. Having seen all he needed to confirm his suspicions, he slid the phone back into her purse. When he looked up, he met her stare.

"Alright," he said, "so where do we go from here?"

What do you mean?" she asked.

"Well you obviously are smitten with him, and my guess is you were planning on a physical encounter after dinner with him this evening. Where does this leave us? Where does this leave me? You remember me, right? Your husband? The guy sitting at home waiting on you - longing for you while you're out throwing yourself at a young buff detective."

Her eyes rocked side to side rapidly before looking back into his stare.

"I'm sorry, Alex," she started. "I don't like when things aren't good between us."

He continued to stare at her as he could feel his heart racing. "When was the last time we had an argument?"

She thought for several minutes. "Maybe 10 years ago. It was before we bought this house."

"Do you remember what it was about?" he inquired.

"No," she said, shaking her head from side to side. "I don't."

"We've gotten along really well for 10 years," he noted.

"Yes," she hastily replied. "You are a wonderful man. My best friend. You know me like no one else. You dote on me. You check on me. You're there for me."

"So then, why?" he asked. "Why would you cheat on me if I treat you so well?"

She turned her eyes away from his stare.

"I don't want to hurt you."

"A little too late for that, isn't it?" he asked.

"I'm sorry. I never wanted to hurt you."

He ran his fingers through his hair.

"You convinced me to love again after I had given up on love. You proposed to me and convinced me that my heart was safe with you," he explained. "Now you're running around on me?"

"It hurts to admit it," she started, "but I enjoyed his attention."

"I see," he replied, "so you're going to throw away our marriage and our relationship to pursue a fantasy."

She dropped her head and then looked back up at him, engaging his stare.

"I'm sorry," she repeated. "I never wanted to hurt you."

Alex stood up from where he was sitting on the edge of the bed beside her and walked out of the bedroom. Colleen laid down on their bed and after what seemed like hours, she finally fell asleep.

Colleen awoke around 5 AM. When she turned over, she realized Alex had never come to bed. She crawled out of bed, slipped on a fluffy robe, and walked through the house. She checked his office, the guest room, and the living room. He was nowhere to be found. She walked back to their bedroom and reviewed the top of his dresser and nightstand. His cell phone, keys, and wallet were gone. His wedding ring sat alone in the middle of the top of the dresser. She walked out the back door and to the carport behind the house to discover his pickup was gone. She hung her head and slowly walked back into the house feeling the full weight of what she had done to their relationship and to him.

She grabbed her cell phone from the charger as she walked back in the house and sent a text to Lori.

"Alex has left. He discovered some of my messages with the detective and got upset. I don't know what I am going to do."

G ary sat at a conference table directly across from his captain and two other detectives.

"Explain to me again what you were doing at Carrabba's with one of the suspects in this case and how she ended up shooting your assailant," Captain Adams demanded.

Gary rubbed his face with both hands and looked up to meet his stare. "I had dinner with Mrs. Smithwick. I was trying to determine what level of involvement, if any, she might have in any of the recent deaths of lenders at her bank. To date, I have noted her animosity towards the two dead lenders but have been unable to connect any evidence to her."

He stopped to take a long sip of coffee from a Starbucks paper cup and continued, "As we were leaving the establishment, I was accosted by an assailant that has now been positively identified as Daryl Levine, the former computer support technician for the bank. As I struggled with the assailant, Mrs. Smithwick drew her weapon and delivered two shots center mass. We have confirmed that she has a valid concealed carry permit. And all of the statements that the other detectives have gathered confirmed she shot the armed assailant in my defense, which is clearly a justifiable use of deadly force."

"I don't have any questions regarding her use of deadly force," Captain Adams stated. "In fact, I plan to ask the mayor's office to give her a commendation for saving the life of one of our officers. What I am concerned about is any improprieties that may exist between you and Mrs. Smithwick. The department doesn't need a black eye from some public revelation that you are having an affair with a possible suspect, and a married one at that."

Gary shook his head in disagreement. "No inappropriate relationship exists between myself and Mrs. Smithwick," he emphatically stated in his own defense.

"Yet!" Captain Adams interjected. "There is no inappropriate relationship yet. But somehow I get this nagging feeling that if the late Mr. Levine had not interrupted your evening, that might not have been the case."

Gary could feel himself blush. "No inappropriate relationship exists with Mrs. Smithwick," he repeated.

"Alright," Captain Adams replied, "what have we got on the motive for Mr. Levine's assault on you?"

A heavy set, balding detective wearing a Tommy Bahama silk shirt sitting at the table instantly chimed in, "After searching his apartment, we found a diary Mr. Levine had been keeping. It appears Mr. Levine had a secret crush on Mrs. Smithwick. He made several entries regarding how some of the lenders mistreated her and his thoughts on intervening on her behalf. Some of those entries indicated that he was considering assaulting a couple of the lenders including the two who died over the last several days. One of the last entries discussed his observations of Detective Black and Mrs. Smithwick. It would appear Mr. Levine concluded that a romantic relationship of some sort was forming between the two, and he was determined to end it. From reading his diary and from comments he made during the attack, we have concluded that he felt threatened by Detective Black as a rival suitor and elected to eliminate him."

"Well isn't that interesting," the captain noted. "Still going with 'no inappropriate relationship exists', Gary?"

Gary nodded. "Yes, sir. That's my story, and I'm sticking to it."

"Fair enough," the captain responded. "Any further investigation into Mrs. Smithwick's possible involvement in any of these cases and any further interviews going forward will be handled by Bernie then. You do not have any further contact with her unless Bernie is present with you. Understood?"

Gary glanced across the table at the heavy set detective and then back at his captain. "Yes, sir. Crystal clear."

"Alright, moving right along," the captain continued. "What have we got on the two lender deaths so far?"

Gary looked up, still deflated from the dressing down he just endured. "Theoretically, Mr. Levine could be the suspect in both of the lender's deaths. After reading that diary, I would nominate him for 'most likely to kill anyone that crossed Colleen'...I mean Mrs. Smithwick's path. I'm reviewing the inventory report and photographs from Mr. Levine's apartment to see if it provides any further clues."

Bernie spoke up, "Honestly the entire loan processing department would have motive to kill either of the two lenders for harsh treatment. No one interviewed denied they disliked them, and several were rather animated in their distaste for both men. We're trying to secure a court order to investigate a Human Resources issue between one of the dead lenders and Margaret Prescott, one of the loan processors. It seems she had reported him a couple times to their H.R. department for abusive behavior. This morning we learned that her late husband died under questionable circumstances in North Georgia about five years ago."

Captain Adams titled his head. "Questionable circumstances?"

Bernie nodded. "Well, the coroner's report states he died at 52 years of age due to natural causes. But his family has been raising a stink ever since his death for an extensive autopsy. They believe there was foul play. The coroner's office and the sheriff's department there do not feel like they have justifiable evidence or probable cause to exhume the body and conduct an autopsy."

Captain Adams stared at a whiteboard on the wall. "The autopsy on the second dead guy revealed ethyl glycol poisoning, correct?"

Bernie nodded again. "Yep. Someone had laced his beloved Mountain Dews with antifreeze. We conducted a search of the desks at the bank for hypodermics and anything that might connect one of the loan processors to that activity but came up with scratch."

Captain Adams nodded. "But what if one of their late husbands died from the same thing five years prior? I'm just spit-balling, mind you.

But what if? I mean, if she got away with it once, would she be tempted to try it again 5 years later in another state?"

Bernie shot a glance at Gary. "That would certainly put a whole new slant on things, wouldn't it?"

Gary raised his eyebrows. "Want me to follow up with that sheriff's office?"

"Yeah, I think you should have a talk with them and their coroner's office. If that type of poisoning might go undetected without a toxicology report, maybe this might give them some motivation to look back into that case a bit deeper. At present, we don't have enough to justify a search of Ms. Prescott's home or car, but if they found her late husband died from ethyl glycol poisoning, I would venture to say one of our judges would consider that an appropriate amount of probable cause to search her house and car. What about the guy that got stabbed in the neck with a letter opener? Have we narrowed down any suspects on that one?"

Gary spoke up. "When we reviewed the parking lot camera from the bank, we discovered that the crime scene was 20-30 feet out of the camera's range. But this morning, I found the auto part store across the street had cameras in their parking lot. One of which has a clear shot of the crime scene from a distance. They've agreed to send us their video tapes of that morning and the night prior. The crime lab will process them once we receive them."

"Good deal," Captain Adams commented. "Alright, y'all are dismissed. Get to work and for God's sake, don't have an affair with a possible suspect. OK?"

Gary hung his head as the captain walked out of the conference room. He looked at his watch. It was 5 AM. He hadn't slept in over 18 hours and decided a hot shower and a nap was probably in order. He walked back to his office and surveyed the messages on his desk. He rubbed his eyes and looked up at Bernie.

"I'm going to go home and get a few hours of sleep. I'll check back in later this afternoon," he said.

Bernie nodded. "Sounds good. I'll call if anything comes up in the meantime."

A lex sat quietly drinking a large WaWa coffee carefully scanning the apartment complex for movement. He had been sitting in his pickup for hours backed into a parking space with a clear view of the parking lot and of the entrance of the apartment building he was surveilling. He glanced at his watch and figured his cover of darkness would soon be lost.

Suddenly, a flash of light beamed from one end of the parking lot. A car was approaching. Alex leaned back against his reclined seat to hide his profile behind the rear edge of the pickup's door frame while attempting to identify the car. As it drew closer, he confirmed it was a Camaro. He waited until the car pulled into a parking space directly in front of the apartment building. Confident that his presence had not been detected, he quietly opened the truck door and stepped out. He pushed the truck door closed without latching it to avoid making any noise that might draw unwanted attention.

Alex noted the driver's focus was firmly set on his destination and not scanning his surroundings. He quietly crept up to the back bumper of the Camaro. The driver was now at the front bumper.

"Good morning, lover boy," Alex called out to him.

He saw the driver freeze in place and reach for his waistband.

"I don't think you need to pull your service weapon, pretty boy. Aren't you supposed to be a lover and not a fighter?" he asked.

Gary slowly turned to face him.

A shot rang out and struck Gary in the shoulder, and he collapsed beside the Camaro. Pain rushed through his shoulder and arm as he tried to make sense out of what was happening. He was injured in his shooting arm and instantly realized he could not manage to get his right hand to retrieve his pistol. He felt his heart thumping in panic as he anticipated Alex's attack.

Gary closed his eyes waiting for the next shot that he expected to pierce his chest. His mind flashed to the bullet proof vest casually tossed in the back seat of the Camaro providing him no protection at all when he needed it the most.

"Great," he thought. "Great. Detective killed by jealous husband. Nothing like going out as a hero."

Suddenly Gary heard another shot. He opened his eyes and looked around. What was happening? He didn't feel another bullet. He looked up and could see the stars. His mind began to process the events. The second shot sounded deeper and louder than the first. Were there two shooters? Did Alex have multiple weapons? He sat himself up with his left arm to survey his surroundings. He saw Alex standing at the trunk of the Camaro. What was he staring at? Alex sprinted across the parking lot. Gary could hear his movements but struggled to understand what was happening. He thought he heard someone kick something.

Gary managed to pull himself to a standing position with his left arm. He dug at his waistband with his left hand and finally managed to retrieve his own gun.

"Alright, Alex," he commanded, "drop your weapons and walk to me with your hands where I can see them."

"Wow!" Alex replied. "You really are a thankless prick aren't you?"

Alex ejected the magazine from his .40 glock and laid it on the hood of his truck. He cycled the slide to eject the live round in the chamber and laid the cartridge and the glock on the hood as well. He raised his hands above his head, turned slowly to face Gary, and stared at him.

"Now, whatcha wanna do? Bleed to death or can I call you some help?" Alex asked.

"What?" Gary responded.

"Well, with one hand I don't think you can hold me at gunpoint and call the calvary. So, can I call 911 for you?" Alex asked.

Still confused about the events that had just taken place, Gary considered Alex's point.

"Fine," he answered. "Slowly retrieve your cell phone."

Alex pulled his cell phone from the holster on his belt and dialed 911. He put the phone on speaker and held it out to Gary.

"Here, you talk to them," he suggested.

Within minutes, a dozen police cars, an ambulance, and a fire department rescue squad descended on their location. Alex was handcuffed and pushed into the backseat of a police SUV.

Paramedics hastily loaded Gary into the ambulance and sped to the emergency room.

Colleen was feverishly trying to complete three rush loan packages when her cell phone rang. She glanced at the notification to see it was Alex calling. She swiped her finger across the face of the phone and answered the call.

"Good morning, dear."

"Well, I guess depending on one's perspective, it is," Alex replied dryly.

"Excuse me?" Colleen asked.

"Long story, but could you come pick me up from the police headquarters?"

Colleen raised her eyebrows.

"Should I even ask?"

"Like I said - long story, but they aren't pressing any charges. My truck is at an apartment complex, and it's too far to walk. Could you help me out?"

Colleen batted her eyelashes rapidly.

"Back up, cowboy. What apartment complex? What did you do last night? What have you gotten into?"

"Colleen, I will explain it all to you, but could you come down here and pick me up, please?" he begged.

"Alright. Alright. Let me finish a couple things, and I will be on my way," she replied.

Colleen hung up her cell phone, grabbed her desk phone, and dialed Elena.

"Elena, I need to step out of the office for a few minutes to pick up Alex. He's having car trouble. I have those three packages ready for review," she hurriedly explained.

Elena approved her break, and Colleen dashed out of the bank.

When she pulled up in front of the police headquarters, Alex was standing at the edge of the sidewalk. He opened the passenger door and crawled into the car.

"Alright," Colleen started, "'splain."

Alex chuckled. "Well, after our conversation last night. I took a little trip over to Mr. Black's apartment complex and waited for him to come home. I wanted to have a little discussion with him."

Colleen's head snapped to look him in the eye.

"More like you wanted to beat his ass."

"Accurate," Alex replied, "but before I had the opportunity, someone across the parking lot shot him in the shoulder and dropped him like a sack of taters."

Colleen's eyes widened. "Holy hell!"

"I managed to get a clear shot and nailed the shooter center mass. I have spent the better part of the morning discussing why I was in the parking lot and my intentions with half of the police department. Apparently the pretty boy detective is in some pretty hot water over y'alls little romance and his captain so much as said that he deserved a good ass whipping."

Colleen shook her head.

"Have they identified the shooter?"

Alex nodded. "Funny thing. He apparently was one of your co-workers at the bank. One Santiago Lopez."

Colleen quietly nodded. "Well that blows the top off of this whole little party."

Alex cocked his head. "What?"

Colleen held up her hand as she began to pull out of the parking lot.

"I'll explain as I drive, but there has been a lot that has gone down the last few weeks that aren't exactly as they seem. Santiago has a lot of eyes on him."

When Colleen arrived back at the bank, the parking lot was full of cars with government license plates. She parked and hurriedly walked up stairs. The second floor was a sea of men and women in blue vests with various agencies' names on the back: FBI, Treasury, and Police, who were collecting files and boxing them. Colleen walked directly into the boardroom where the lead investigators were gathered. A treasury agent dressed in a suit with a badge hanging from a cord around his neck glanced up as she walked into the room.

"Welcome, Colleen. As you are aware, Santiago Lopez attempted to conduct a hit on a local detective this morning," the agent began. "We were about to begin briefing the local police on the case we have building against him with your assistance."

Colleen looked to Captain Adams, Detective Black's supervisor. "Captain Adams, several months ago, I became very suspicious of the numerous offshore mortgages for Colombian tree farms that Santiago was bringing into the bank. All of the loans were to LLCs either formed in Delaware, Nevada, or Wyoming or formed in a country known to be lacking in effective money laundering controls. I began providing information to the Financial Crimes Enforcement Network, a bureau of the United States Department of the Treasury."

The treasury agent then took over the briefing. "When we reviewed the initial information that Mrs. Smithwick provided, we immediately contacted the FBI due to our concerns with the other known exports from Columbia and other active money laundering cases. We tasked Mrs. Smithwick with determining who all within the bank had knowledge of the loans and the loan originators. We have determined that the bank president, and two other loan officers besides Santiago had knowledge of the actual money laundering involved that these loans were used to provide some apparent legitimacy. It is our belief that Brad Stuckey and Richard Shiver had intimate knowledge of the actors involved and the actual purposes of the mortgages. It is our belief that they became uncomfortable with the number of mortgages and put pressure on Santiago to either end the activities or that they were going to go to authorities, and so he murdered both of the men to secure their silence. We further believe that Santiago became nervous of the investigation that Detective Black was conducting and attempted to kill him to remove him from his trail."

Captain Adams smirked. "Detective Black has had a couple attempts on his general welfare over the last few days. Mrs. Smithwick shot and killed one attacker and her husband shot and killed the second. I have to wonder if perhaps I should dismiss him and hire them."

The treasury agent grinned. "Our investigators noted they both seem to be very proficient with firearms. Along with the FBI, we are collecting files for the cases we are making against those involved that are still alive. We'll be happy to share any information you deem relevant to your homicide investigations. Unless you have any further questioning for her, we are not holding Mrs. Smithwick."

Captain Adams shook his head. "No. The mayor has recommended that she and her husband both receive accommodations from the city on behalf of the police department for protecting the life of one of our officers."

He looked directly at Colleen. "Ma'am, we greatly appreciate your cooperation with this case and your quick action to spare the life of one of our detectives."

Colleen smiled. "You're welcome."

Several days later, Alex and Colleen attended a presentation at city hall by the mayor and the police chief. Both were presented keys to the city and proclamations for their actions in saving the life of a city police officer. Pictures were taken by local newspapers, interviews were held by local television channels. Numerous city police officers and city council members greeted them.

After the presentation, as they were walking across the parking lot to their car, Detective Gary Black met them.

"I just wanted to thank you both again for saving my life," he started. He looked at Alex and extended his right hand. "No hard feelings?"

Alex grasped his right hand, as to shake it, and then hit him squarely across the bridge of the nose with his left fist. Pain shot through Gary's face, his teeth ached, and blood shot out of his nose. He cupped his nose as he fell to his knees. He quickly righted himself and looked up to Alex's stare.

"I guess I deserved that," he said.

"Damn right you did," Alex answered. "Think about that every time you ever consider bedding a married woman in the future."

Alex retrieved a white handkerchief from his jacket pocket and tossed it to the detective.

"Here, clean yourself up. You're a mess," he said before turning and walking back to the car where Colleen stood trying to contain her shock at the sudden outbreak of violence she had never before witnessed from her husband.

They drove home to their charming Florida cottage in silence. As they walked into the house, Colleen opened the refrigerator.

"Would you like a Mountain Dew?" she asked.

"Sure. Thanks," Alex replied.

He didn't remember them stocking the house with sugar based soda but didn't give it much thought.

Allen Madding

# Other Books by Allen Madding

## **Volunteer Management 101:**
## **How to Recruit and Retain Volunteers**
### by Allen Madding and Dan King

An employee needs the paycheck to pay the rent, the mortgage, the car payment, student debt, the credit card bill, the utilities, and a host of other bills. Volunteers, on the other hand are not motivated by a paycheck to stick it out when the manger is chewing someone out or things get uncomfortable.

The volunteer is simply motivated by making a difference and being a part of the organization. Their commitment hinges on how vested they are with the vision and purpose of the organization. When it gets to be too much of a hassle to serve, when they feel unappreciated, or when they feel the commitment is too demanding, they will walk away – usually without any warning or explanation.

With several decades of experience between them, Madding and King share insights on how to manage these valuable resources in your organization.

## Shaken Awake: The Complete Trilogy

by Allen Madding

A dreadful chill ravages the city and a homeless man is found frozen to death on the church steps…

The city of Atlanta had weathered a thousand wet and chilly days in winter with occasional snowfall… but never one like this. A snowfall that begins in the noon turns into a vicious ice storm by evening, obliterating everything in its way. People are stuck into the whiteout, and trying to look for a way out.

Now, as the Peachtree Church opens its door to those out in cold, the church members come face to face with a stark reality.

As uncomfortable truths make themselves known, this storm will prove be to an eye opener for many.

Enlightening and compelling, Shaken Awake brings to surface a truth we either ignore or just don't know. With richly textured characters, haunted by the memories of their past, Shaken Awake is both a deeply engrossing novel and a thought-provoking piece of social commentary.

ABOUT THE AUTHOR

Allen Madding is a follower of the way, author, traveler, Atlanta Braves and Dallas Cowboys fan, and an information technology professional who lives in St. Petersburg, Florida. He grew up in rural South Georgia where he developed a love for hunting, fishing, putting peanuts in a Coca-Cola, and racing cars. He raced short track stock cars for nine years and has written for Speedway Media and Insider Racing News. He is a retired volunteer firefighter/NREMT-I and fancies himself as a storyteller and a guitar strummer.

He is always up for a road trip and a hot cup of truck stop coffee. He feels at home in wide open spaces, hiking in the woods, walking on the beach listening to the ocean's tide, watching the sunset over a cypress lined pond, and relishes the smell of honeysuckle and the sound of the wind through the pines.

He loves a medium rare steak, cheeseburgers, blackberry cobbler, bourbon and Coke, boiled peanuts from a roadside stand, a hotdog and beer at a baseball game while heckling the opposing team and keeping the umpire honest. He roots for the underdog and has learned how to say "I'm sorry". He believes that Dale Earnhardt was the greatest driver to ever compete in NASCAR, that Chevrolet is the heartbeat of America, and that Ford is a four letter word.

He says "Yes, Sir" and "No Ma'am" and prays before a meal. He believes that scars are the original tattoos and has a collection of both that remind him where he has been and help to keep him headed in the right direction.

www.ingramcontent.com/pod-product-compliance
Lightning Source LLC
Chambersburg PA
CBHW060047150626
46556CB00018BA/3047